P9-DFX-572

MONSTER NEEDS A PARTY

MONSTER NEEDS A PARTY

Story by **PAUL CZAJAK** *Illustrations by* **WENDY GRIEB**

mighty media KIDS

MINNEAPOLIS, MINNESOTA

Published by Mighty Media Kids, an imprint of Mighty Media Press, a division of Mighty Media, Inc.

Guided Reading Level: O *(Developmental Reading Assessment 34)*

LIBRARY OF CONGRESS CATALOGING-IN-PUBLICATION DATA

Czajak, Paul.
Monster needs a party / by Paul Czajak ; pictures by Wendy Grieb.
pages cm
Summary: Disappointed when none of his friends can attend his pirate birthday party, Monster cheers up when he goes to a pirate theme park, instead.
ISBN 978-1-938063-55-8 (hardcover : alk. paper) -- ISBN 978-1-938063-56-5 (ebook : alk. paper)
[1. Stories in rhyme. 2. Parties--Fiction. 3. Birthdays--Fiction. 4. Monsters--Fiction. 5. Pirates--Fiction.] I. Grieb, Wendy, illustrator. II. Title.
PZ8.3.C9975Mom 2015
[E]--dc23
2014044048

Art Direction and book design by
Anders Hanson, Mighty Media, Inc.

Printed and manufactured in the United States
North Mankato, Minnesota
Distributed by Publishers Group West

10 9 8 7 6 5 4 3 2

PAUL CZAJAK got an F with the words "get a tutor" on his college writing paper and after that, he never thought he'd become a writer. But after spending twenty years as a chemist, he knew his creativity could no longer be contained. Paul lives in New Jersey with his wife and two little monsters. In addition to the Monster & Me™ series, he's also the author of *Seaver the Weaver.*

WENDY GRIEB is an Annie Award-winning storyboard artist, who has worked as a developmental artist, illustrator, and character designer for companies such as Disney, Nickelodeon, Sony, Klasky-Csupo, White Wolf, and more. Wendy lives with her husband and son in California.

Dedication

To Hadley—for your first birthday.

Of course, this means I no longer have to buy you presents. I mean, really, how many kids can say their name is in a book?

Monster needs a party since another year has passed.

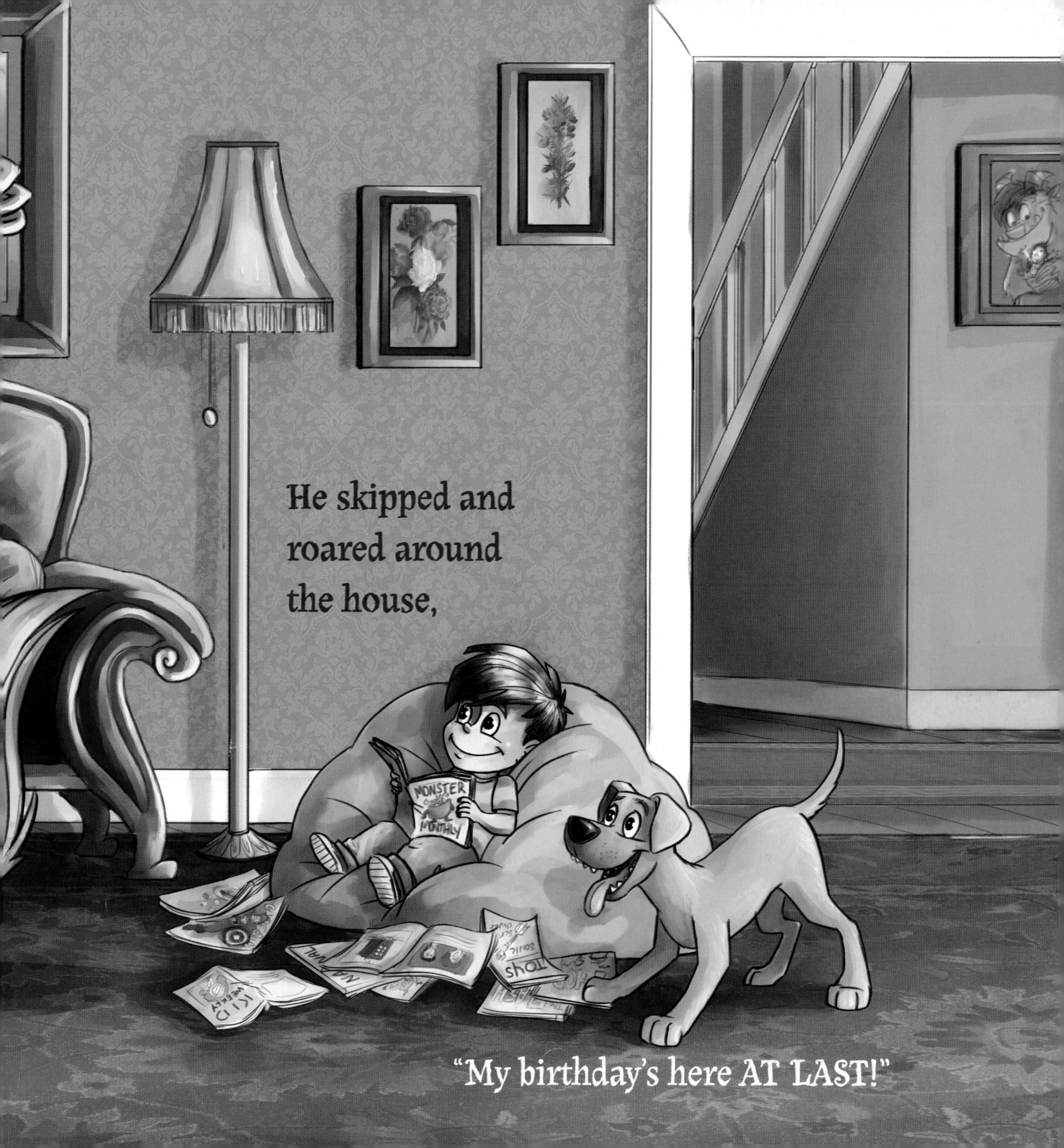

He skipped and roared around the house,

"My birthday's here AT LAST!"

“Let’s celebrate with all my friends and have a pirate party.

With treasure maps and gold doubloons,

we'll have some fun, me-hearty!"

“Monster, we can
decorate with
streamers and
balloons.

And wear a patch,
a pirate hat, and
puffy pantaloons.”

Monster got his party clothes and he was so excited.

I said to him, "I'll phone your friends
and tell them they're invited."

I made the calls to all his pals,
but sadly none could come.

And Monster's
Jolly Roger
started
looking
rather glum.

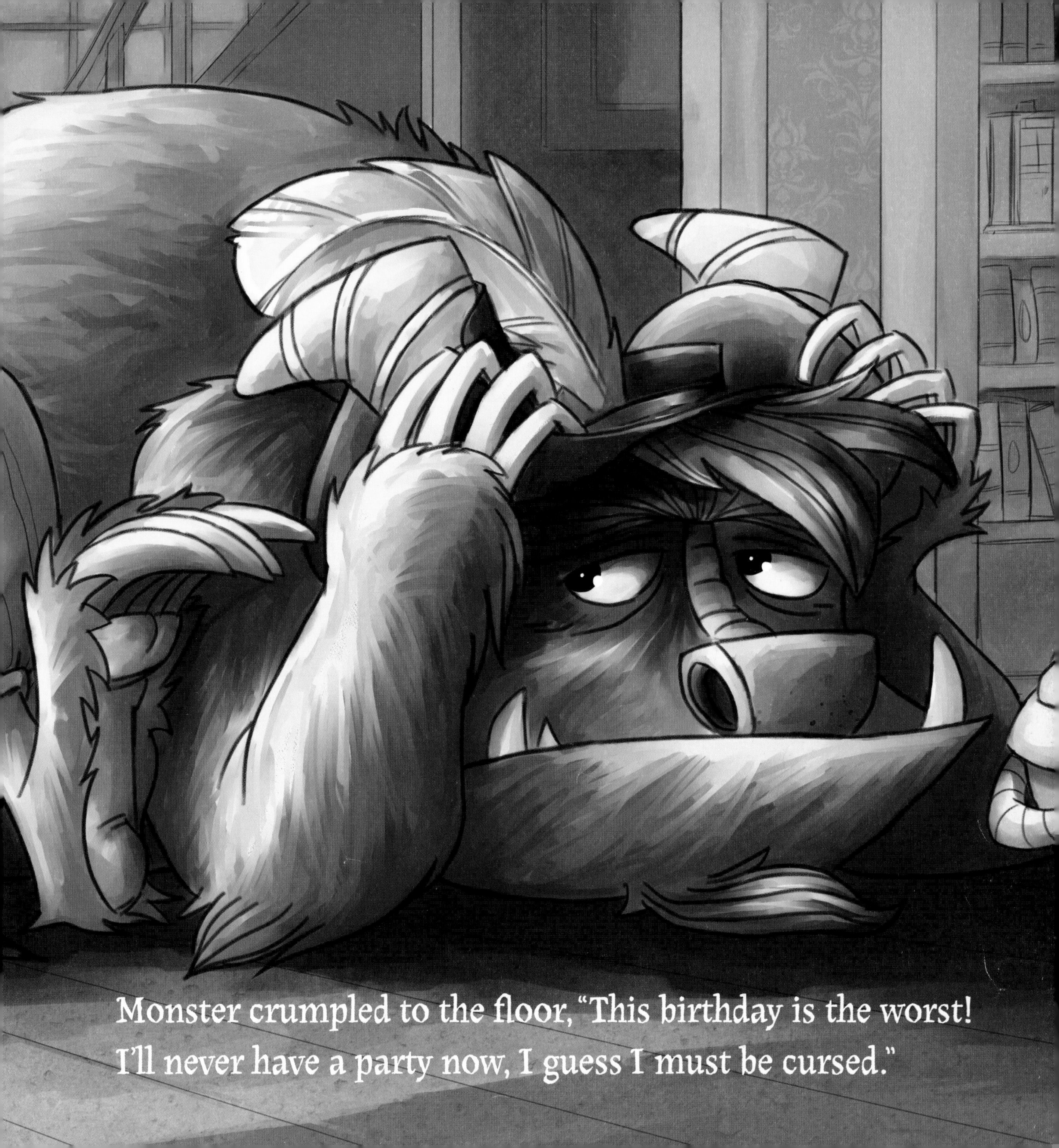

Monster crumpled to the floor, "This birthday is the worst!
I'll never have a party now, I guess I must be cursed."

"Don't be sad, this may not be the birthday you had planned.

But you and I can celebrate and go to Pirate Land."

Monster pouted, sighed, and said, "The theme park sounds okay."

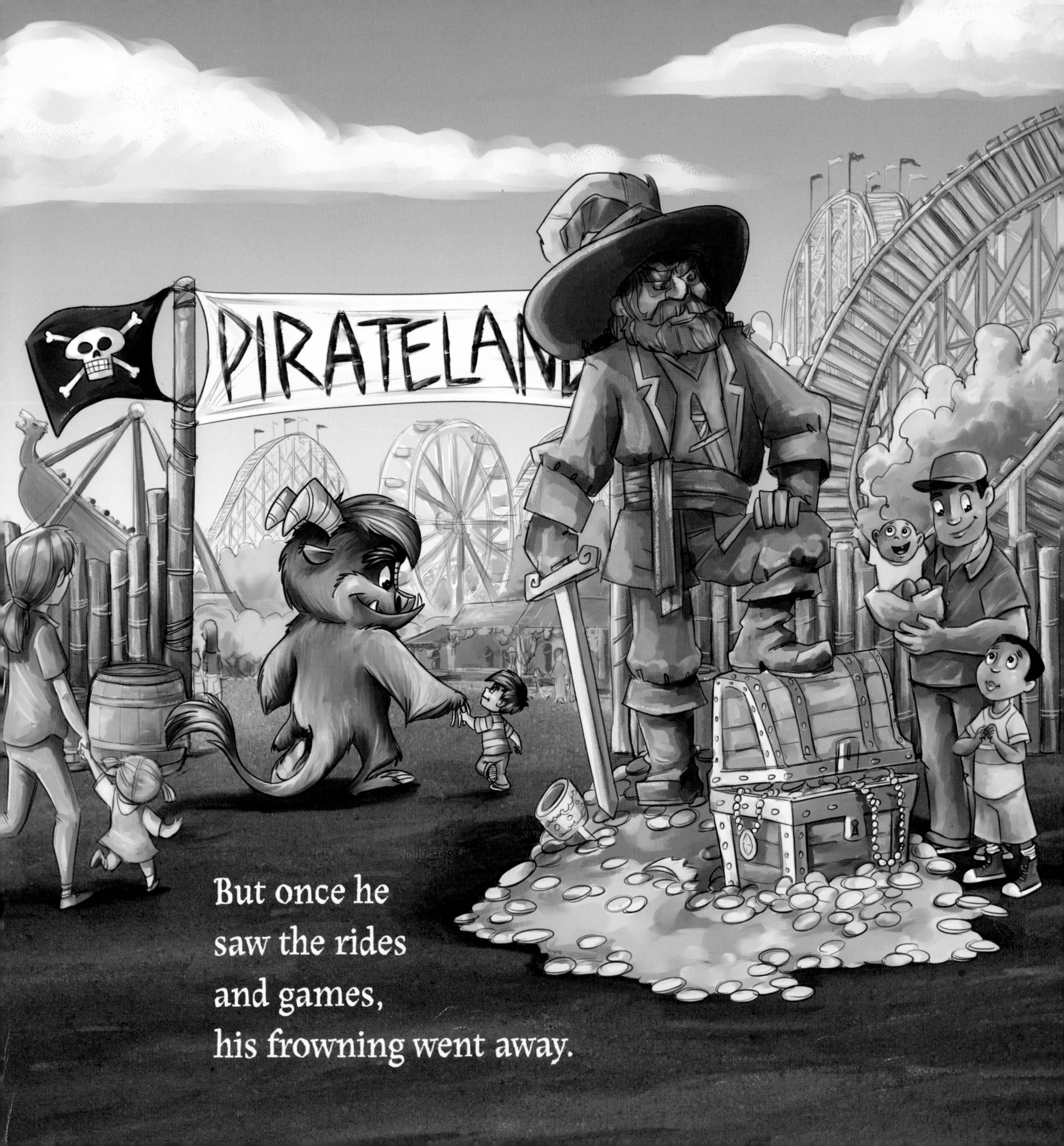

But once he
saw the rides
and games,
his frowning went away.

We rode in Blackbeard's Bumper Cars ...

and Wind's Eye
Ferris Wheel.

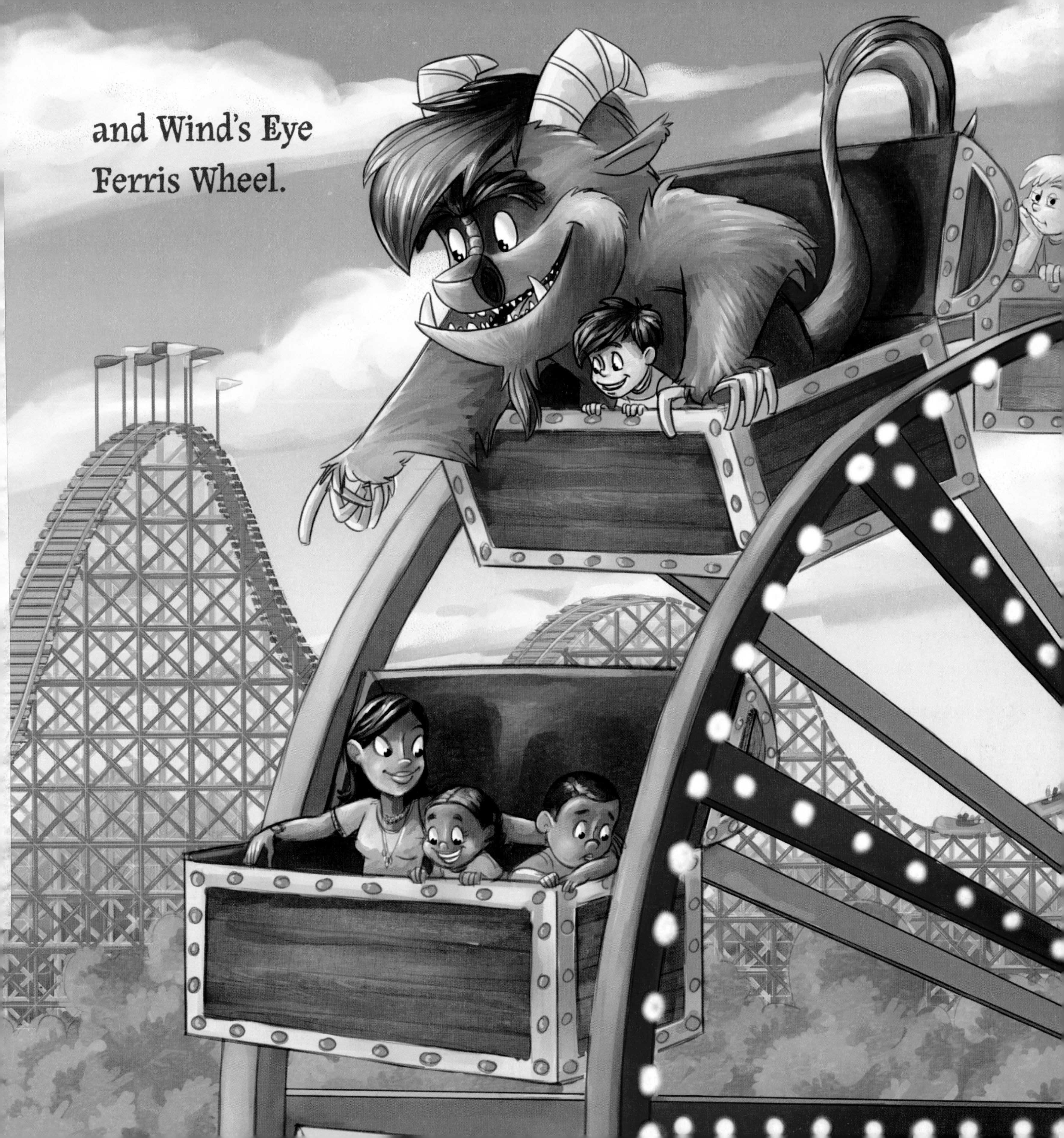

And when we rode the Crossbones Coaster,

Monster gave a ...

SQUEEEEAL!

EXIT

EXIT

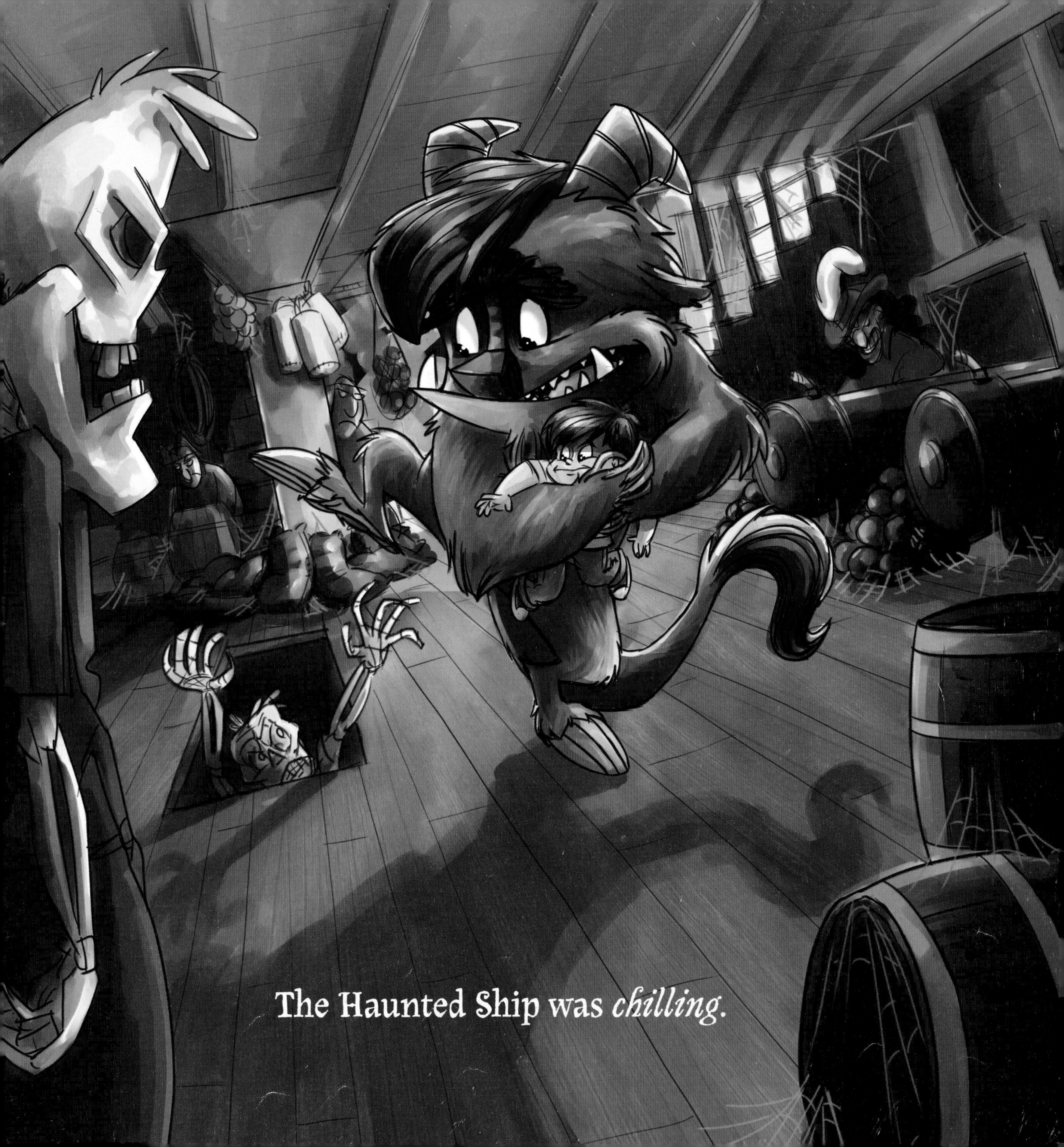

The Haunted Ship was *chilling*.

But Monster smiled throughout it all and thought the rides were thrilling!

Monster said, "Let's play some games and try to win a prize."

But Ring Toss got the best of him

and so did Swat the Flies.

Monster was persistent and was *not* about to quit.

He tossed a ball,
the barrels fell ...

with just a single hit.

"I won the parrot,"
Monster roared.
"The biggest
one of all!"

But next to him that fluffy bird was looking rather small.

Monster had a root beer float,
which filled his face with foam.

And crunched on
candied apples as we made our way back home.

"I had a lot of fun today," Monster said to me.
"Even though there wasn't any pirate jamboree."

When Monster walked into the house, he had to rub his eyes.